Hiccup and the Dragon Riders had
spotted an unknown island kingdom on
a map. They had to fly a long way to find
it. Everyone was very tired.

Then Hiccup saw something in the
distance. It was an island!
"Let's land and rest there,"
he suggested.

DreamWorks DRAGONS

DANGEROUS SONGS

HODDER CHILDREN'S BOOKS

First published by Nelson Verlag, Völckersstraße 14–20, 22765 Hamburg

First published in Great Britain in 2018 by Hodder and Stoughton

A CIP catalogue record for this book
is available from the British Library.

ISBN: 978 1 444 94450 1

Printed and bound in China by RR Donnelley Asia Printing Solutions Limited

The paper and board used in this book are made from wood from responsible sources

MIX
Paper from
responsible sources
FSC® C104740

Hodder Children's Books
An imprint of
Hachette Children's Group
Part of Hodder and Stoughton
Carmelite House
50 Victoria Embankment
London, EC4Y 0DZ

An Hachette UK Company
www.hachette.co.uk

www.hachettechildrens.co.uk

Everyone wanted to explore but Hiccup
said they should get some sleep first.
Snotlout built a fire by using some of
Hookfang's flammable spit.

Early the next morning, Hiccup was
woken by Astrid.
"Our dragons, they're all gone!"

Suddenly they heard a strange sound. "What is that?" Tuffnut wondered. "It almost sounds like singing."

They ran towards it and found what
they were looking for – their dragons!

All around them there were lots
of dragons trapped in a strange
substance. It was hard as rock.

Snotlout rushed to his dragon.
"Hookfang!" he shouted.

But he could not free his friend.

Just then a new
dragon appeared.
It was singing as it
flew over them.

"It must be that dragon!" shouted
Hiccup. "He attracts other dragons with

his singing, then traps them. We should call him the Death Song Dragon!"

Before they could hide, the singing
dragon launched his extra sticky spit
at the friends. Now the Dragon Riders
were stuck too!

The Death Song Dragon had flown away.
Only Hiccup had escaped it and now he
had to free everyone! Luckily he already
had an idea.

Hiccup pulled the jug of flammable spit
out of Hookfang's saddle.

"What are you doing?" asked Snotlout,
as Hiccup poured some liquid onto him.

"Just trust me," replied Hiccup. Then he covered everyone else with Hookfang's explosive spit.

"Okay, nobody move!" Hiccup shouted.
He beat two stones against each other.
Soon sparks appeared and Hookfang's
spit caught fire.

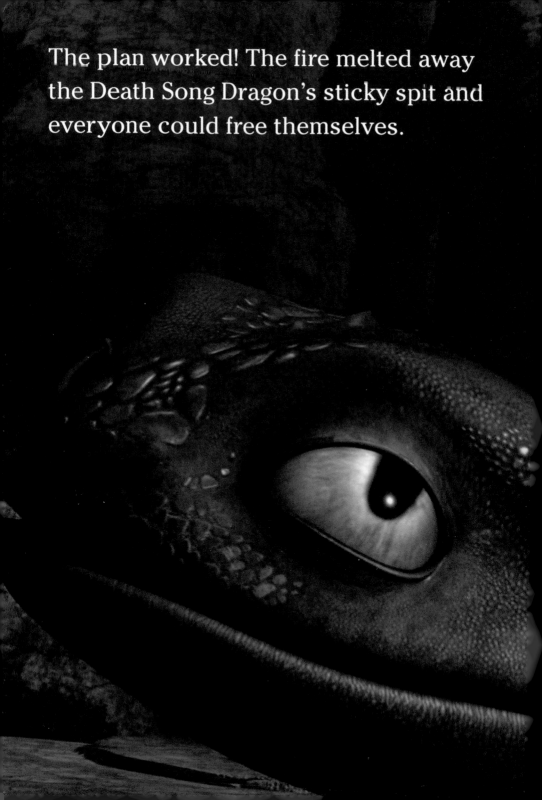

The plan worked! The fire melted away the Death Song Dragon's sticky spit and everyone could free themselves.

Howling wildly, the Death Song Dragon came back.

Hiccup jumped on Toothless's back and flew past the Death Song Dragon. It followed him into a cave. Toothless turned at the last minute and blasted some rocks, trapping the other dragon.

"No one can hear his singing now. The dragons will be safe!"

The other Dragon Riders were relieved
and flew off to their next adventure.